THOMAS & FRIENDS™

HEROIC RAILS

Illustrated by Tommy Stubbs

g A GOLDEN BOOK · NEW YORK

Thomas the Tank Engine & Friends™

CREATED BY BRITT ALLCROFT

Based on The Railway Series by The Reverend W Awdry.
© 2009 Gullane (Thomas) LLC.
Thomas the Tank Engine & Friends and Thomas & Friends are trademarks of Gullane (Thomas) Limited.
HIT and the HIT Entertainment logo are trademarks of HIT Entertainment Limited.
All rights reserved. Published in the United States by Golden Books, an imprint of Random House Children's Books, a division
of Random House, Inc., 1745 Broadway, New York, NY 10019, and in Canada by Random House of Canada Limited, Toronto.
Golden Books, A Golden Book, and the G colophon are registered trademarks of Random House, Inc.
www.randomhouse.com/kids   www.thomasandfriends.com
Library of Congress Cataloging-in-Publication Data is available upon request.
ISBN: 978-0-375-85462-0 (trade) – ISBN: 978-0-375-96179-3 (lib. bdg.)
Printed in the United States of America ♪ 10 9 8 7 6 5 4 3 2 1   First Edition
Random House Children's Books supports the First Amendment and celebrates the right to read.

It was a beautiful summer day on the Island of Sodor. The fields were full of flowers, and the birds sang sweetly in the trees. Thomas felt very happy as he quietly filled up with water.

Suddenly, there was a *whoosh* and a *clickity-clack* as a silver blur roared past him.

"Fizzling fireboxes!" peeped Thomas. "What was that?"

Later that day, Spencer thundered up the track to Knapford Station. All the engines realized who had been roaring around the island.

"I'm here for the summer," Spencer puffed smugly. "I have a very important job to do. The Duke and Duchess of Boxford are having a new summer house built. It has to be finished in time for their holiday."

"Cinders and ashes!" huffed Thomas. "Having Speedy Spencer on Sodor for one day is bad . . . but the whole summer? That will be terrible!"

During the next few days, Spencer was very rude to the other engines. He forced his way onto Gordon's express line. He told Toby he was too old to be useful. And he even called Thomas a tiny toy tank engine!

This was too much! Thomas told Spencer he could pull loads just as heavy as his, so Spencer challenged Thomas to a race around Sodor. They would haul equal loads and see who could go faster.

The engines met at the Shunting Yards at dawn. A whistle wailed, and the race was on! Thomas and Spencer pumped their pistons as they whooshed along the tracks.

As Thomas sped down a big hill, his brakes broke! He rolled faster and faster. He came to an old stretch of overgrown tracks that he'd never seen before and crashed through the bushes.

Finally, he slowed to a stop . . . and then he heard a noise.

"Hello, my name is Hiro," a strange voice said.

There was a very old engine in the bushes. He was rusty and broken. At first, Thomas wanted to roll away as fast as his wheels could carry him. But then he realized that Hiro was kind and gentle.

Hiro told Thomas he had come to Sodor a long, long time ago. He had been one of the first steam engines on Sodor and had been known as the Master of the Railway.

But Hiro had broken down, and there'd been no parts on Sodor to fix him with. He'd waited for parts to come from his home island—but the parts had never arrived. He was forgotten.

Thomas said he would get Sir Topham Hatt to help.

"No!" Hiro cried. "You can't do that. You know what happens to old engines that aren't Really Useful anymore—they're sent to the smelting yard!"

Thomas decided to help his new friend in secret. "I promise I will make you Really Useful again!"

Later, Thomas had his brakes repaired at the Sodor
Steamworks. He liked the hustle and bustle there, and he
especially liked Victor, who managed the whole place.

Thomas wanted to tell everyone about Hiro, but he knew he had to keep quiet. As Thomas chuffed away, he spotted an old engine part that Kevin the Crane had dropped. "This will be good for Hiro," he thought, and puffed away excitedly.

The next day, Thomas did his work quickly and then sped
out to visit Hiro. As he neared Hiro's hiding place, Thomas
made a terrible discovery!

"Cinders and ashes!" he peeped. "The Duke and Duchess's
summer house is right next to Hiro's hiding place. Spencer
will be here every day!"

Thomas knew he had to be careful.

Just then, Spencer steamed around the bend. "What are you doing here?" he asked. "I think you're up to something." Thomas didn't answer. He just chuffed away nervously.

Thomas knew he couldn't do his work *and* repair Hiro on his own. So he went to Percy and told him everything.

"Of course I'll help," Percy peeped. "What can I do?"

"Will you take this tractor to Farmer McColl for me?" Thomas asked.

Percy was excited about helping Thomas, but first he had to find a place to hide his mail trucks. He would deliver the mail after he took care of the tractor for Thomas.

Percy found an old siding to hide the mail trucks in, then went off with the tractor. But the tractor was so heavy that Percy popped a valve!

Percy had to be repaired at the Sodor Steamworks. And in all the excitement he forgot where he had hidden the mail trucks.

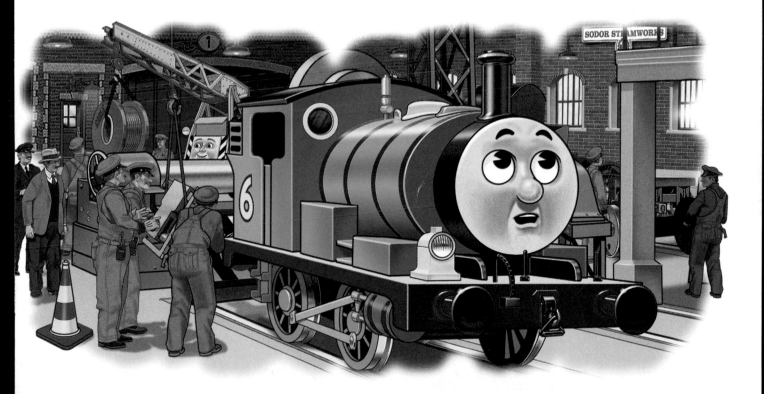

Back at Tidmouth Sheds, Sir Topham Hatt was very cross that Percy had lost his mail trucks. His voice boomed through the station, from the top to the tracks.

"I'm sorry, sir," Thomas peeped. "I can help Percy find them tomorrow."

Thomas' friends knew something strange was going on, so he told them all about Hiro. Gordon gasped. James jumped. They had never heard such an amazing story!

The next morning, Thomas was a Really Useful Engine. He huffed and puffed, and he never stopped to rest his axles. And the whole time, he knew Spencer was following him.

Suddenly, an idea flew into Thomas' funnel! If Spencer was going to follow him all day, he could lead that nosy engine away from Hiro. That would mean all the other engines would be free to help repair him.

The next day, Thomas and Percy looked for the mail trucks as far away from Hiro as possible. They puffed out to the Quarry . . . with Spencer sneaking behind them the whole way.

When they got there, Mavis wouldn't leave Spencer alone.

"What an honor!" she puffed. "Let me take you around the Quarry!"

As he toured the Quarry, Spencer biffed a hopper. Slate and dust showered down and blocked his funnel! Edward had to pull him to the Works to be repaired.

With Spencer at the Works, Thomas thought it was a good time to take his friends to visit Hiro.

Hiro liked meeting the other engines. He enjoyed Emily's stories and admired James' shiny red paint. But making all these new friends reminded him of old friends back home, which made him sad.

"Don't worry," Thomas peeped. "Tomorrow Percy will bring the last part. Then you'll be ready—and you won't be alone anymore!"

The next morning, Spencer found Percy's missing mail
trucks near Hiro's hiding placc!

"These must be part of Tricky Thomas' tricks!" he huffed,
then raced back to Knapford Station to find Sir Topham
Hatt.

"Spencer, why did you take Percy's mail trucks?" Sir
Topham Hatt demanded.

"I didn't take . . ."

Sir Topham Hatt wasn't interested in Spencer's excuses.
He just wanted Spencer to return the trucks to Percy and
get back to his work on the summer house.

Spencer was mad. "I won't let Thomas get away with this!"

Thomas and Hiro were waiting for Percy to bring the very last part. Hiro was very excited. His firebox flared and his steam swirled.

But then they heard Spencer coming down the track. "I've found you," he huffed.

"Hiro, you can puff away from him!" Thomas steamed. "Let's go!"

With a heaving huff, Hiro tried to race away. But without the missing piece, his pistons couldn't pump. His engine juddered and jittered. Metal parts popped off him, and he sputtered to a stop.

Spencer laughed. "Is this what you've been doing, Thomas? Making a heap of metal for the smelting yard? Sir Topham Hatt will make sure he's sent there!"

As Spencer steamed away, Thomas felt terrible. Everything he had promised Hiro was ruined. He knew he had to find Sir Topham Hatt before Spencer did.

Thomas and Spencer had the race of their lives. They steamed through tunnels and roared around bends.

But as they crossed over a marsh, Spencer realized he was too heavy for the old track. It creaked and cracked! Then the mighty Spencer slid into the muddy marsh. Thomas promised Spencer he'd get help.

At Knapford Station, Thomas found Sir Topham Hatt with the Duke and Duchess. Thomas' wheels wobbled as he told them all about Hiro.

Sir Topham Hatt was shocked. "You mean you found the Master of the Railway?"

"He's terribly famous!" exclaimed the Duchess.

"Why didn't you come to me sooner?" Sir Topham Hatt asked Thomas.

"I was worried, so I tried to do it all alone," Thomas peeped.

"Well, you're not alone," said Sir Topham Hatt. "We must help Hiro at once!"

A few days later, all the engines went to see Hiro at the Sodor Steamworks. When he puffed up the track, they couldn't believe their eyes. He looked wonderful—as good as new!

"Welcome back, Master of the Railway!" said Sir Topham Hatt. All the engines blew their whistles.

"Now go get Spencer out of the mud," Sir Topham Hatt said.

Together with Rocky and Thomas, Hiro pulled Spencer from the mud. Spencer couldn't believe how shiny and new Hiro looked!

"I'm sorry I thought you were a tricky engine, Thomas," puffed Spencer. "And I'm sorry I called you a heap of scrap, Hiro."

With a mighty heave and haul, Hiro pulled Spencer all the way to the Works.

Spencer, Thomas, and Hiro huffed and puffed and worked together on the summer house. The Duke and Duchess arrived for their holiday just as it was finished—and they were delighted!

Later, as they were resting their axles, Thomas noticed that Hiro was sad.

"What's the matter, Hiro?" Thomas asked.

"You have been very kind, the best friend I could ever have," Hiro huffed. "But I want to go home."

Thomas knew who could help Hiro, and he went to find Sir Topham Hatt at Knapford Station.

"Sir, I need your help," he said. "Hiro wants to go home. He misses his friends and his island."

"Thomas, you were right to ask me," Sir Topham Hatt said. "Tell Hiro not to worry."

A few days later, all the engines gathered at Brendam Docks to say goodbye to Hiro. Flags and garlands fluttered in the breeze. It was time for Hiro to go home.

"I will never forget what you did for me," Hiro said to Thomas. "And I'll never forget you."

"Sodor will always be your home, too, Hiro," Thomas puffed happily.

As Hiro chuffed slowly to the ship, all the engines whistled farewell to their friend, the Master of the Railway.